Love in the Night

F. Scott Fitzgerald

A Phoenix Paperback

This collection first published in Great Britain by Phoenix
A division of Orion Books Ltd
Orion House, 5 Upper St Martin's Lane, London WC2H 9EA

'Love in the Night' first appeared in the
Saturday Evening Post in March 1925;
'The Swimmers' first appeared in the
Saturday Evening Post in October 1929.

ISBN 1 85799 603 8

Typeset at The Spartan Press Ltd,
Lymington, Hants
Printed in Great Britain by
Clays Ltd, St Ives plc

CONTENTS

Love in the Night

The words thrilled Val. They had come into his mind sometime during the fresh gold April afternoon and he kept repeating them to himself over and over: 'Love in the night; love in the night.' He tried them in three languages – Russian, French and English – and decided that they were best in English. In each language they meant a different sort of love and a different sort of night – the English night seemed the warmest and softest with a thinnest and most crystalline sprinkling of stars. The English love seemed the most fragile and romantic – a white dress and a dim face above it and eyes that were pools of light. And when I add that it was a French night he was thinking about, after all, I see I must go back and begin over.

Val was half Russian and half American. His mother was the daughter of that Morris Hasylton who helped finance the Chicago World's Fair in 1892, and his father was – see the *Almanach de Gotha*, issue of 1910 – Prince Paul Serge Boris Rostoff, son of Prince Vladimir Rostoff, grandson of a grand duke – 'Jimber-jawed Serge' – and third-cousin-once-removed to the czar. It was all very impressive, you see, on that side – house in St Petersburg, shooting lodge near Riga, and swollen villa, more like a palace, overlooking the Mediterranean. It was at this villa in Cannes that the Rostoffs passed the winter – and it wasn't at all the thing to remind Princess Rostoff that this Riviera villa, from the marble fountain – after Bernini – to the gold cordial glasses – after dinner – was paid for with American gold.

The Russians, of course, were gay people on the Continent in the gala days before the war. Of the three races that used Southern France for a pleasure ground they were easily the most adept at the grand manner. The English were too practical, and the Americans, though they spent freely, had no tradition of romantic conduct. But the Russians – there was a people as gallant as the Latins, and rich besides! When the Rostoffs arrived at Cannes late in January the restaurateurs telegraphed north for the Prince's favorite labels to paste on their champagne, and the jewelers put incredibly gorgeous articles aside to show him – but not to the princess – and the Russian Church was swept and garnished for the season that the Prince might beg orthodox forgiveness for his sins. Even the Mediterranean turned obligingly to a deep wine color in the spring evenings, and fishing boats with robin-breasted sails loitered exquisitely offshore.

In a vague way young Val realized that this was all for the benefit of him and his family. It was a privileged paradise, this white little city on the water, in which he was free to do what he liked because he was rich and young and the blood of Peter the Great ran indigo in his veins. He was only seventeen in 1914, when this history begins, but he had already fought a duel with a young man four years his senior, and he had a small hairless scar to show for it on top of his handsome head.

But the question of love in the night was the thing nearest his heart. It was a vague pleasant dream he had, something that was going to happen to him some day that would be unique and incomparable. He could have told no more about it than that there was a lovely unknown girl concerned in it, and that it ought to take place beneath the Riviera moon.

The odd thing about all this was not that he had this excited and yet almost spiritual hope of romance, for all boys of any imagination have just such hopes, but that it actually came true. And when it happened, it happened so unexpectedly; it was such a jumble of impressions and emotions, of curious phrases that sprang to his lips, of sights and sounds and moments that were here, were lost, were past, that he scarcely understood it at all. Perhaps its very vagueness preserved it in his heart and made him forever unable to forget.

There was an atmosphere of love all about him that spring – his father's loves, for instance, which were many and indiscreet, and which Val became aware of gradually from overhearing the gossip of servants, and definitely from coming on his American mother unexpectedly one afternoon, to find her storming hysterically at his father's picture on the salon wall. In the picture his father wore a white uniform with a furred dolman and looked back impassively at his wife as if to say 'Were you under the impression, my dear, that you were marrying into a family of clergymen?'

Val tiptoed away, surprised, confused – and excited. It didn't shock him as it would have shocked an American boy of his age. He had known for years what life was among the Continental rich, and he condemned his father only for making his mother cry.

Love went on around him – reproachless love and illicit love alike. As he strolled along the seaside promenade at nine o'clock, when the stars were bright enough to compete with the bright lamps, he was aware of love on every side. From the open-air cafés, vivid with dresses just down from Paris, came a sweet pungent odor of flowers and chartreuse and fresh black coffee and cigarettes – and mingled with them all he caught another scent, the mysterious thrilling scent of love. Hands touched jewel-sparkling hands upon the white tables. Gay dresses and white shirt fronts swayed together, and matches were held, trembling a little, for slow-lighting cigarettes. On the other side of the boulevard lovers less fashionable, young Frenchmen who worked in the stores of Cannes, sauntered with their fiancées under the dim trees, but Val's young eyes seldom turned that way. The luxury of music and bright colors and low voices – they were all part of his dream. They were the essential trappings of Love in the night.

But assume as he might the rather fierce expression that was expected from a young Russian gentleman who walked the streets alone, Val was beginning to be unhappy. April twilight had succeeded March twilight, the season was almost over, and he had found no use to make of the warm spring evenings. The girls of sixteen and seventeen whom he knew, were chaperoned with care between dusk and bedtime – this, remember, was before the war – and the others who might gladly have walked beside him were an affront to his romantic desire. So April passed by – one week, two weeks, three weeks —

He had played tennis until seven and loitered at the courts for another hour, so it was half-past eight when a tired cab horse accomplished the hill on which gleamed the façade of the Rostoff villa. The lights of his mother's limousine were yellow in the drive, and the princess, buttoning her gloves, was just coming out the glowing door. Val tossed two francs to the cabman and went to kiss her on the cheek.

'Don't touch me,' she said quickly. 'You've been handling money.'

'But not in my mouth, mother,' he protested humorously.

The princess looked at him impatiently.

'I'm angry,' she said. 'Why must you be so late tonight? We're dining on a yacht and you were to have come along too.'

'What yacht?'

'Americans.' There was always a faint irony in her voice when she mentioned the land of her nativity. Her America was the Chicago of the nineties which she still thought of as the vast upstairs to a butcher shop. Even the irregularities of Prince Paul were not too high a price to have paid for her escape.

'Two yachts,' she continued; 'in fact we don't know which one. The note was very indefinite. Very careless indeed.'

Americans. Val's mother had taught him to look down on Americans, but she hadn't succeeded in making him dislike them. American men noticed you, even if you were seventeen. He liked Americans. Although he was thoroughly Russian he wasn't immaculately so – the exact proportion, like that of a celebrated soap, was about ninety-nine and three-quarters per cent.

'I want to come,' he said, 'I'll hurry up, mother. I'll —'

'We're late now.' The princess turned as her husband appeared in the door. 'Now Val says he wants to come.'

'He can't,' said Prince Paul shortly. 'He's too outrageously late.'

Val nodded. Russian aristocrats, however indulgent about themselves, were always admirably Spartan with their children. There were no arguments.

'I'm sorry,' he said.

Prince Paul grunted. The footman, in red and silver livery, opened the limousine door. But the grunt decided the matter for Val, because Princess Rostoff at that day and hour had certain grievances against her husband which gave her command of the domestic situation.

'On second thought you'd better come, Val,' she announced coolly. 'It's too late now, but come after dinner. The yacht is either the Minnehaha or the Privateer.' She got into the limousine. 'The one to come to will be the gayer one, I suppose – the Jacksons' yacht —'

'Find got sense,' muttered the Prince cryptically, conveying that Val would find it if he had any sense. 'Have my man take a look at you 'fore you start. Wear tie of mine 'stead of that outrageous string you affected in Vienna. Grow up. High time.'

As the limousine crawled crackling down the pebbled drive Val's face was burning.

II

It was dark in Cannes harbor, rather it seemed dark after the brightness of the promenade that Val had just left behind. Three frail dock lights glittered dimly upon innumerable fishing boats heaped like shells along the beach. Farther out in the water there were other lights where a fleet of slender yachts rode the tide with slow dignity, and farther still a full ripe moon made the water bosom into a polished dancing floor. Occasionally there was a swish! creak! drip! as a rowboat moved about in the shallows, and its blurred shape threaded the labyrinth of hobbled fishing skiffs and launches. Val, descending the velvet slope of sand, stumbled over a sleeping boatman and caught the rank savor of garlic and plain wine. Taking the man by the shoulders he shook open his startled eyes.

'Do you know where the Minnehaha is anchored, and the Privateer?'

As they slid out into the bay he lay back in the stern and stared with vague discontent at the Riviera moon. That was the right moon, all right. Frequently, five nights out of seven, there was the right moon. And here was the soft air, aching with enchantment, and here was the music, many strains of music from many orchestras, drifting out from the shore. Eastward lay the dark Cape of Antibes, and then Nice, and beyond that Monte Carlo, where the night rang chinking full of gold. Some day he would enjoy all that, too, know its every pleasure and success – when he was too old and wise to care.

But tonight – tonight, that stream of silver that waved like a wide strand of curly hair toward the moon; those soft romantic lights of Cannes behind him, the irresistible ineffable love in this air – that was to be wasted forever.

'Which one?' asked the boatman suddenly.

'Which what?' demanded Val, sitting up.

'Which boat?'

He pointed. Val turned; above hovered the gray, sword-like prow of a yacht. During the sustained longing of his wish they had covered half a mile.

He read the brass letters over his head. It was the Privateer, but there were only dim lights on board, and no music and no voices, only a murmurous k-plash at intervals as the small waves leaped at the sides.

'The other one,' said Val; 'the Minnehaha.'

'Don't go yet.'

Val started. The voice, low and soft, had dropped down from the darkness overhead.

'What's the hurry?' said the soft voice. 'Thought maybe somebody was coming to see me, and have suffered terrible disappointment.'

The boatman lifted his oars and looked hesitatingly at Val. But Val was silent, so the man let the blades fall into the water and swept the boat out into the moonlight.

'Wait a minute!' cried Val sharply.

'Good-by,' said the voice. 'Come again when you can stay longer.'

'But I am going to stay now,' he answered breathlessly.

He gave the necessary order and the rowboat swung back to the foot of the small companionway. Someone young, someone in a misty white dress, someone with a lovely low voice, had actually called to him out of the velvet dark. 'If she has eyes!' Val murmured to himself. He liked the romantic sound of it and repeated it under his breath – 'If she has eyes.'

'What are you?' She was directly above him now; she was looking down and he was looking up as he climbed the ladder, and as their eyes met they both began to laugh. 9

She was very young, slim, almost frail, with a dress that accentuated her youth by its blanched simplicity. Two wan dark spots on her cheeks marked where the color was by day.

'What are you?' she repeated, moving back and laughing again as his head appeared on the level of the deck. 'I'm frightened now and I want to know.'

'I am a gentleman,' said Val, bowing.

'What sort of gentleman? There are all sorts of gentlemen. There was a – there was a colored gentleman at the table next to ours in Paris, and so —' She broke off. 'You're not American, are you?'

'I'm Russian,' he said, as he might have announced himself to an archangel. He thought quickly and then added, 'And I am the most fortunate of Russians. All this day, all this spring I have dreamed of falling in love on such a night, and now I see that heaven has sent me to you.'

'Just one moment!' she said, with a little gasp. 'I'm sure now that this visit is a mistake. I don't go in for anything like that. Please!'

'I beg your pardon.' He looked at her in bewilderment, unaware that he had taken too much for granted. Then he drew himself up formally.

'I have made an error. If you will excuse me I will say good night.'

He turned away. His hand was on the rail.

'Don't go,' she said, pushing a strand of indefinite hair out of her eyes. 'On second thoughts you can talk any nonsense you like if you'll only not go. I'm miserable and I don't want to be left alone.'

Val hesitated; there was some element in this that he failed to understand. He had taken it for granted that a girl who called to a strange man at night, even from the deck of a yacht, was certainly in a mood for romance. And he wanted intensely to stay. Then he remembered that this was one of the two yachts he had been seeking.

'I imagine that the dinner's on the other boat,' he said.

'The dinner? Oh, yes, it's on the Minnehaha. Were you going there?'

'I was going there – a long time ago.'

'What's your name?'

He was on the point of telling her when something made him ask a question instead.

'And you? Why are you not at the party?'

'Because I preferred to stay here. Mrs Jackson said there would be some Russians there – I suppose that's you.' She looked at him with interest. 'You're a very young man, aren't you?'

'I am much older than I look,' said Val stiffly. 'People always comment on it. It's considered rather a remarkable thing.'

'How old are you?'

'Twenty-one,' he lied.

She laughed.

'What nonsense! You're not more than nineteen.'

His annoyance was so perceptible that she hastened to

reassure him. 'Cheer up! I'm only seventeen myself. I might have gone to the party if I'd thought there'd be anyone under fifty there.'

He welcomed the change of subject.

'You preferred to sit and dream here beneath the moon.'

'I've been thinking of mistakes.' They sat down side by side in two canvas deck chairs. 'It's a most engrossing subject – the subject of mistakes. Women very seldom brood about mistakes – they're much more willing to forget than men are. But when they do brood —'

'You have made a mistake?' inquired Val.

She nodded.

'Is it something that cannot be repaired?'

'I think so,' she answered. 'I can't be sure. That's what I was considering when you came along.'

'Perhaps I can help in some way,' said Val. 'Perhaps your mistake is not irreparable, after all.'

'You can't,' she said unhappily. 'So let's not think about it. I'm very tired of my mistake and I'd much rather you'd tell me about all the gay, cheerful things that are going on in Cannes tonight.'

They glanced shoreward at the line of mysterious and alluring lights, the big toy banks with candles inside that were really the great fashionable hotels, the lighted clock in the old town, the blurred glow of the Café de Paris, the pricked-out points of villa windows rising on slow hills toward the dark sky.

'What is everyone doing there?' she whispered. 'It looks as though something gorgeous was going on, but what it is I can't quite tell.'

'Everyone there is making love,' said Val quietly.

'Is that it?' She looked for a long time, with a strange expression in her eyes. 'Then I want to go home to America,' she said. 'There is too much love here. I want to go home tomorrow.'

'You are afraid of being in love then?'

She shook her head.

'It isn't that. It's just because – there is no love here for me.'

'Or for me either,' added Val quietly. 'It is sad that we two should be at such a lovely place on such a lovely night and have – nothing.'

He was leaning toward her intently, with a sort of inspired and chaste romance in his eyes – and she drew back.

'Tell me more about yourself,' she inquired quickly. 'If you are Russian where did you learn to speak such excellent English?'

'My mother was American,' he admitted. 'My grandfather was American also, so she had no choice in the matter.'

'Then you're American too!'

'I am Russian,' said Val with dignity.

She looked at him closely, smiled and decided not to argue. 'Well then,' she said diplomatically. 'I suppose you must have a Russian name.'

But he had no intention now of telling her his name. A name, even the Rostoff name, would be a desecration of the night. They were their own low voices, their two white faces – and that was enough. He was sure, without any reason for being sure but with a sort of instinct that sang triumphantly through his mind, that in a little while, a minute or an hour, he was going to undergo an initiation into the life of romance. His name had no reality beside what was stirring in his heart.

'You are beautiful,' he said suddenly.

'How do you know?'

'Because for women moonlight is the hardest light of all.'

'Am I nice in the moonlight?'

'You are the loveliest thing that I have ever known.'

'Oh.' She thought this over. 'Of course I had no business to let you come on board. I might have known what we'd talk about – in this moon. But I can't sit here and look at the shore – forever. I'm too young for that. Don't you think I'm too young for that?'

'Much too young,' he agreed solemnly.

Suddenly they both became aware of new music that was close at hand, music that seemed to come out of the water not a hundred yards away.

'Listen!' she cried. 'It's from the Minnehaha. They've finished dinner.'

For a moment they listened in silence.

'Thank you,' said Val suddenly.

'For what?'

He hardly knew he had spoken. He was thanking the deep low horns for singing in the breeze, the sea for its warm murmurous complaint against the bow, the milk of the stars for washing over them until he felt buoyed up in a substance more taut than air.

'So lovely,' she whispered.

'What are we going to do about it?'

'Do we have to do something about it? I thought we could just sit and enjoy —'

'You didn't think that,' he interrupted quietly. 'You know that we must do something about it. I am going to make love to you – and you are going to be glad.'

'I can't,' she said very low. She wanted to laugh now, to make some light cool remark that would bring the situation back into the safe waters of a casual flirtation. But it was too late now. Val knew that the music had completed what the moon had begun.

'I will tell you the truth,' he said. 'You are my first love. I am seventeen – the same age as you, no more.'

There was something utterly disarming about the fact that they were the same age. It made her helpless before the fate that had thrown them together. The deck chairs creaked and he was conscious of a faint illusive perfume as they swayed suddenly and childishly together.

Whether he kissed her once or several times he could not afterward remember, though it must have been an hour that they sat there close together and he held her hand. What surprised him most about making love was that it seemed to have no element of wild passion – regret, desire, despair – but a delirious promise of such happiness in the world, in living, as he had never known. First love – this was only first love! What must love itself in its fullness, its perfection be. He did not know that what he was experiencing then, that unreal, undesirous medley of ecstasy and peace, would be unrecapturable forever.

The music had ceased for some time when presently the murmurous silence was broken by the sound of a rowboat disturbing the quiet waves. She sprang suddenly to her feet and her eyes strained out over the bay.

'Listen!' she said quickly. 'I want you to tell me your name.'

'No.'

'Please,' she begged him. 'I'm going away tomorrow.'

He didn't answer.

'I don't want you to forget me,' she said. 'My name is —'

'I won't forget you. I will promise to remember you always. Whoever I may love I will always compare her to you, my first love. So long as I live you will always have that much freshness in my heart.'

'I want you to remember,' she murmured brokenly. 'Oh, this has meant more to me than it has to you – much more.'

She was standing so close to him that he felt her warm young breath on his face. Once again they swayed together. He pressed her hands and wrists between his as it seemed right to do, and kissed her lips. It was the right kiss, the romantic kiss – not too little or too much. Yet there was a sort of promise in it of other kisses he might have had, and it was with a slight sinking of his heart that he heard the rowboat close to the yacht and realized that her family had returned. The evening was over.

'And this is only the beginning,' he told himself. 'All my life will be like this night.'

She was saying something in a low quick voice and he was listening tensely.

'You must know one thing – I am married. Three months ago. That was the mistake that I was thinking about when the moon brought you out here. In a moment you will understand.'

She broke off as the boat swung against the companionway and a man's voice floated up out of the darkness.

'Is that you, my dear?'

'Yes.'

'What is this other rowboat waiting?'

'One of Mrs Jackson's guests came here by mistake and I made him stay and amuse me for an hour.'

17

A moment later the thin white hair and weary face of a man of sixty appeared above the level of the deck. And then Val saw and realized too late how much he cared.

IV

When the Riviera season ended in May the Rostoffs and all the other Russians closed their villas and went north for the summer. The Russian Orthodox Church was locked up and so were the bins of rarer wine, and the fashionable spring moonlight was put away, so to speak, to wait for their return.

'We'll be back next season,' they said as a matter of course.

But this was premature, for they were never coming back any more. Those few who straggled south again after five tragic years were glad to get work as chambermaids or *valets de chambre* in the great hotels where they had once dined. Many of them, of course, were killed in the war or in the revolution; many of them faded out as spongers and small cheats in the big capitals, and not a few ended their lives in a sort of stupefied despair.

When the Kerensky government collapsed in 1917, Val was a lieutenant on the eastern front, trying desperately to enforce authority in his company long after any vestige of it remained. He was still trying when Prince Paul Rostoff and his wife gave up their lives one rainy morning to atone for the blunders of the Romanoffs – and the enviable career of Morris Hasylton's daughter ended in a city that bore even more resemblance to a butcher shop than had Chicago in 1892.

After that Val fought with Denikin's army for a while until he realized that he was participating in a hollow farce and the glory of Imperial Russia was over. Then he went to France and was suddenly confronted with the astounding problem of keeping his body and soul together.

It was, of course, natural that he should think of going to America. Two vague aunts with whom his mother had quarreled many years ago still lived there in comparative affluence. But the idea was repugnant to the prejudices his mother had implanted in him, and besides he hadn't sufficient money left to pay for his passage over. Until a possible counter-revolution should restore to him the Rostoff properties in Russia he must somehow keep alive in France.

So he went to the little city he knew best of all. He went to Cannes. His last two hundred francs bought him a third-class ticket and when he arrived he gave his dress suit to an obliging party who dealt in such things and received in return money for food and bed. He was sorry afterward that he had sold the dress suit, because it might have helped him to a position as a waiter. But he obtained work as a taxi driver instead and was quite as happy, or rather quite as miserable, at that.

Sometimes he carried Americans to look at villas for

rent, and when the front glass of the automobile was up, curious fragments of conversation drifted out to him from within.

'— heard this fellow was a Russian prince.' . . . 'Sh!' . . . 'No, this one right here.' . . . 'Be quiet, Esther!' — followed by subdued laughter.

When the car stopped, his passengers would edge around to have a look at him. At first he was desperately unhappy when girls did this; after a while he didn't mind any more. Once a cheerfully intoxicated American asked him if it were true and invited him to lunch, and another time an elderly woman seized his hand as she got out of the taxi, shook it violently and then pressed a hundred-franc note into his hand.

'Well, Florence, now I can tell 'em back home I shook hands with a Russian prince.'

The inebriated American who had invited him to lunch thought at first that Val was a son of the czar, and it had to be explained to him that a prince in Russia was simply the equivalent of a British courtesy lord. But he was puzzled that a man of Val's personality didn't go out and make some real money.

'This is Europe,' said Val gravely. 'Here money is not made. It is inherited or else it is slowly saved over a period of many years and maybe in three generations a family moves up into a higher class.'

'Think of something people want — like we do.'

'That is because there is more money to want with in

America. Everything that people want here has been thought of long ago.'

But after a year and with the help of a young Englishman he had played tennis with before the war, Val managed to get into the Cannes branch of an English bank. He forwarded mail and bought railroad tickets and arranged tours for impatient sight-seers. Sometimes a familiar face came to his window; if Val was recognized he shook hands; if not he kept silence. After two years he was no longer pointed out as a former prince, for the Russians were an old story now – the splendor of the Rostoffs and their friends was forgotten.

He mixed with people very little. In the evenings he walked for a while on the promenade, took a slow glass of beer in a café, and went early to bed. He was seldom invited anywhere because people thought that his sad, intent face was depressing – and he never accepted anyhow. He wore cheap French clothes now instead of the rich tweeds and flannels that had been ordered with his father's from England. As for women, he knew none at all. Of the many things he had been certain about at seventeen, he had been most certain about this – that his life would be full of romance. Now after eight years he knew that it was not to be. Somehow he had never had time for love – the war, the revolution and now his poverty had conspired against his expectant heart. The springs of his emotion which had first poured forth one April night had dried up immediately and only a faint trickle remained.

His happy youth had ended almost before it began. He saw himself growing older and more shabby, and living always more and more in the memories of his gorgeous boyhood. Eventually he would become absurd, pulling out an old heirloom of a watch and showing it to amused young fellow clerks who would listen with winks to his tales of the Rostoff name.

He was thinking these gloomy thoughts one April evening in 1922 as he walked beside the sea and watched the never-changing magic of the awakening lights. It was no longer for his benefit, that magic, but it went on, and he was somehow glad. Tomorrow he was going away on his vacation, to a cheap hotel farther down the shore where he could bathe and rest and read; then he would come back and work some more. Every year for three years he had taken his vacation during the last two weeks in April, perhaps because it was then that he felt the most need for remembering. It was in April that what was destined to be the best part of his life had come to a culmination under a romantic moonlight. It was sacred to him – for what he had thought of as an initiation and a beginning had turned out to be the end.

He paused now in front of the Café des Étrangers and after a moment crossed the street on impulse and sauntered down to the shore. A dozen yachts, already turned to a beautiful silver color, rode at anchor in the bay. He had seen them that afternoon, and read the names painted on their bows – but only from habit. He had done it for three years now, and it was almost a natural function of his eye.

'*Un beau soir*,' remarked a French voice at his elbow. It was a boatman who had often seen Val here before. 'Monsieur finds the sea beautiful?'

'Very beautiful.'

'I too. But a bad living except in the season. Next week, though, I earn something special. I am paid well for simply waiting here and doing nothing more from eight o'clock until midnight.'

'That's very nice,' said Val politely.

'A widowed lady, very beautiful, from America, whose yacht always anchors in the harbor for the last two weeks in April. If the Privateer comes tomorrow it will make three years.'

V

All night Val didn't sleep – not because there was any question in his mind as to what he should do, but because his long stupefied emotions were suddenly awake and alive. Of course he must not see her – not he, a poor failure with a name that was now only a shadow – but it would make him a little happier always to know that she remembered. It gave his own memory another dimension, raised it like those stereopticon glasses that bring out a picture from the flat paper. It made him sure that he had

23

not deceived himself – he had been charming once upon a time to a lovely woman, and she did not forget.

An hour before train time next day he was at the railway station with his grip, so as to avoid any chance encounter in the street. He found himself a place in a third-class carriage of the waiting train.

Somehow as he sat there he felt differently about life – a sort of hope, faint and illusory, that he hadn't felt twenty-four hours before. Perhaps there was some way in these next few years in which he could make it possible to meet her once again – if he worked hard, threw himself passionately into whatever was at hand. He knew of at least two Russians in Cannes who had started over again with nothing except good manners and ingenuity and were now doing surprisingly well. The blood of Morris Hasylton began to throb a little in Val's temples and made him remember something he had never before cared to remember – that Morris Hasylton, who had built his daughter a palace in St Petersburg, had also started from nothing at all.

Simultaneously another emotion possessed him, less strange, less dynamic but equally American – the emotion of curiosity. In case he did – well, in case life should ever make it possible for him to seek her out, he should at least know her name.

He jumped to his feet, fumbled excitedly at the carriage handle and jumped from the train. Tossing his valise into the check room he started at a run for the American consulate.

'A yacht came in this morning,' he said hurriedly to a clerk, 'an American yacht – the Privateer. I want to know who owns it.'

'Just a minute,' said the clerk, looking at him oddly. 'I'll try to find out.'

After what seemed to Val an interminable time he returned.

'Why, just a minute,' he repeated hesitantly. 'We're – it seems we're finding out.'

'Did the yacht come?'

'Oh, yes – it's here all right. At least I think so. If you'll just wait in that chair.'

After another ten minutes Val looked impatiently at his watch. If they didn't hurry he'd probably miss his train. He made a nervous movement as if to get up from his chair.

'Please sit still,' said the clerk, glancing at him quickly from his desk. 'I ask you. Just sit down in that chair.'

Val stared at him. How could it possibly matter to the clerk whether or not he waited?

'I'll miss my train,' he said impatiently. 'I'm sorry to have given you all this bother —'

'Please sit still! We're glad to get it off our hands. You see, we've been waiting for your inquiry for – ah – three years.'

Val jumped to his feet and jammed his hat on his head.

'Why didn't you tell me that?' he demanded angrily.

'Because we had to get word to our – our client. Please don't go! It's – ah, it's too late.'

25

Val turned. Someone slim and radiant with dark frightened eyes was standing behind him, framed against the sunshine of the doorway.

'Why —'

Val's lips parted, but no words came through. She took a step toward him.

'I —' She looked at him helplessly, her eyes filling with tears. 'I just wanted to say hello,' she murmured. 'I've come back for three years just because I wanted to say hello.'

Still Val was silent.

'You might answer,' she said impatiently. 'You might answer when I'd – when I'd just about begun to think you'd been killed in the war.' She turned to the clerk. 'Please introduce us!' she cried. 'You see, I can't say hello to him when we don't even know each other's names.'

It's the thing to distrust these international marriages, of course. It's an American tradition that they always turn out badly, and we are accustomed to such headlines as: 'Would Trade Coronet for True American Love, Says Duchess,' and 'Claims Count Mendicant Tortured Toledo Wife.' The other sort of headlines are never printed, for who would want to read: 'Castle is Love Nest, Asserts Former Georgia Belle,' or 'Duke and Packer's Daughter Celebrate Golden Honeymoon.'

So far there have been no headlines at all about the young Rostoffs. Prince Val is much too absorbed in that string of moonlight-blue taxicabs which he manipulates with such unusual efficiency, to give out interviews. He and his wife only leave New York once a year – but there is still a boatman who rejoices when the Privateer steams into Cannes harbor on a mid-April night.

The Swimmers

In the Place Benoît, a suspended mass of gasoline exhaust cooked slowly by the June sun. It was a terrible thing, for, unlike pure heat, it held no promise of rural escape, but suggested only roads choked with the same foul asthma. In the offices of The Promissory Trust Company, Paris Branch, facing the square, an American man of thirty-five inhaled it, and it became the odor of the thing he must presently do. A black horror suddenly descended upon him, and he went up to the washroom, where he stood, trembling a little, just inside the door.

Through the washroom window his eyes fell upon a sign — 1000 Chemises. The shirts in question filled the shop window, piled, cravated and stuffed, or else draped with shoddy grace on the show-case floor. 1000 Chemises — Count them! To the left he read Papeterie, Pâtisserie, Solde, Réclame, and Constance Talmadge in Déjeuner de Soleil; and his eye, escaping to the right, met yet more somber announcements: Vêtements Ecclésiastiques, Déclaration de Décès, and Pompes Funèbres. Life and death.

Henry Marston's trembling became a shaking; it would be pleasant if this were the end and nothing more need be done, he thought, and with a certain hope he sat down on a stool. But it is seldom really the end, and after a while, as he became too exhausted to care, the shaking stopped and he was better. Going downstairs, looking as alert and self-possessed as any other officer of the bank, he spoke to two clients he knew, and set his face grimly toward noon.

'Well, Henry Clay Marston! A handsome old man shook hands with him and took the chair beside his desk.

'Henry, I want to see you in regard to what we talked about the other night. How about lunch? In that green little place with all the trees.'

'Not lunch, Judge Waterbury; I've got an engagement.'

'I'll talk now, then; because I'm leaving this afternoon. What do these plutocrats give you for looking important around here?'

Henry Marston knew what was coming.

'Ten thousand and certain expense money,' he answered.

'How would you like to come back to Richmond at about double that? You've been over here eight years and you don't know the opportunities you're missing. Why both my boys —'

Henry listened appreciatively, but this morning he couldn't concentrate on the matter. He spoke vaguely about being able to live more comfortably in Paris and restrained himself from stating his frank opinion upon existence at home.

Judge Waterbury beckoned to a tall, pale man who stood at the mail desk.

'This is Mr Wiese,' he said. 'Mr Wiese's from downstate; he's a halfway partner of mine.'

'Glad to meet you, suh.' Mr Wiese's voice was rather too deliberately Southern. 'Understand the judge is makin' you a proposition.'

'Yes,' Henry answered briefly. He recognized and detested the type – the prosperous sweater, presumably evolved from a cross between carpetbagger and poor white. When Wiese moved away, the judge said almost apologetically:

'He's one of the richest men in the South, Henry.' Then, after a pause: 'Come home, boy.'

'I'll think it over, judge.' For a moment the gray and ruddy head seemed so kind; then it faded back into something one-dimensional, machine-finished, blandly and bleakly un-European. Henry Marston respected that open kindness – in the bank he touched it with daily appreciation, as a curator in a museum might touch a precious object removed in time and space; but there was no help in it for him; the questions which Henry Marston's life propounded could be answered only in France. His seven generations of Virginia ancestors were definitely behind him every day at noon when he turned home.

Home was a fine high-ceiling apartment hewn from the palace of a Renaissance cardinal in the Rue Monsieur – the sort of thing Henry could not have afforded in America. Choupette, with something more than the rigid tradition-alism of a French bourgeois taste, had made it beautiful, and moved through gracefully with their children. She was a frail Latin blonde with fine large features and vividly sad French eyes that had first fascinated Henry in a Grenoble *pension* in 1918. The two boys took their looks from Henry, voted the handsomest man at the University of Virginia a few years before the war.

Climbing the two broad flights of stairs, Henry stood panting a moment in the outside hall. It was quiet and cool here, and yet it was vaguely like the terrible thing that was going to happen. He heard a clock inside his apartment strike one, and inserted his key in the door.

The maid who had been in Choupette's family for thirty years stood before him, her mouth open in the utterance of a truncated sigh.

'*Bonjour*, Louise.'

'Monsieur!' He threw his hat on a chair. 'But, monsieur – but I thought monsieur said on the phone he was going to Tours for the children!'

'I changed my mind, Louise.'

He had taken a step forward, his last doubt melting away at the constricted terror in the woman's face.

'Is madame home?'

Simultaneously he perceived a man's hat and stick on the hall table and for the first time in his life he heard silence – a loud, singing silence, oppressive as heavy guns or thunder. Then, as the endless moment was broken by the maid's terrified little cry, he pushed through the portières into the next room.

An hour later Doctor Derocco, *de la Faculté de Médecine*, rang the apartment bell. Choupette Marston, her face a little drawn and rigid, answered the door. For a moment they went through French forms; then:

'My husband has been feeling unwell for some weeks,' she said concisely. 'Nevertheless, he did not complain in a way to make me uneasy. He has suddenly collapsed; he cannot articulate or move his limbs. All this, I must say, might have been precipitated by a certain indiscretion of mine – in all events, there was a violent scene, a discussion, and sometimes when he is agitated, my husband cannot comprehend well in French.'

'I will see him,' said the doctor; thinking: 'Some things are comprehended instantly in all languages.'

During the next four weeks several people listened to strange speeches about one thousand chemises, and heard how all the population of Paris was becoming etherized by cheap gasoline – there was a consulting psychiatrist, not inclined to believe in any underlying mental trouble; there was a nurse from the American Hospital, and there was Choupette, frightened, defiant and, after her fashion, deeply sorry. A month later, when Henry awoke to his familiar room, lit with a dimmed lamp, he found her sitting beside his bed and reached out for her hand.

'I still love you,' he said – 'that's the odd thing.'

'Sleep, male cabbage.'

'At all costs,' he continued with a certain feeble irony, 'you can count on me to adopt the Continental attitude.'

'Please! You tear at my heart.'

When he was sitting up in bed they were ostensibly close together again – closer than they had been for months.

'Now you're going to have another holiday,' said Henry to the two boys, back from the country. 'Papa has got to go to the seashore and get really well.'

'Will we swim?'

'And get drowned, my darlings?' Choupette cried. 'But fancy, at your age. Not at all!'

So, at St Jean de Luz they sat on the shore instead, and watched the English and Americans and a few hardy French pioneers of *le sport* voyage between raft and diving tower, motorboat and sand. There were passing ships, and bright islands to look at, and mountains reaching into cold zones, and red and yellow villas, called Fleur des Bois, Mon Nid, or Sans-Souci; and farther back, tired French villages of baked cement and gray stone.

Choupette sat at Henry's side, holding a parasol to shelter her peach-bloom skin from the sun.

'Look!' she would say, at the sight of tanned American girls. 'Is that lovely? Skin that will be leather at thirty – a sort of brown veil to hide all blemishes, so that everyone will look alike. And women of a hundred kilos in such bathing suits! Weren't clothes intended to hide Nature's mistakes?'

Henry Clay Marston was a Virginian of the kind who are prouder of being Virginians than of being Americans. That mighty word printed across a continent was less to him than the memory of his grandfather, who freed his slaves in '58, fought from Manassas to Appomattox, knew Huxley and Spencer as light reading, and believed in caste only when it expressed the best of race.

To Choupette all this was vague. Her more specific criticisms of his compatriots were directed against the women.

'How would you place them?' she exclaimed. 'Great ladies, bourgeoises, adventuresses – they are all the same. Look! Where would I be if I tried to act like your friend, Madame de Richepin? My father was a professor in a provincial university, and I have certain things I wouldn't do because they wouldn't please my class, my family. Madame de Richepin has other things she wouldn't do because of her class, her family.' Suddenly she pointed to an American girl going into the water: 'But that young lady may be a stenographer and yet be compelled to warp herself, dressing and acting as if she had all the money in the world.'

'Perhaps she will have, some day.'

'That's the story they are told; it happens to one, not to the ninety-nine. That's why all their faces over thirty are discontented and unhappy.'

Though Henry was in general agreement, he could not help being amused at Choupette's choice of target this afternoon. The girl – she was perhaps eighteen – was obviously acting like nothing but herself – she was what his father would have called a thoroughbred. A deep, thoughtful face that was pretty only because of the irrepressible determination of the perfect features to be recognized, a face that could have done without them and not yielded up its poise and distinction.

In her grace, at once exquisite and hardy, she was that perfect type of American girl that makes one wonder if the male is not being sacrificed to it, much as, in the last century, the lower strata in England were sacrificed to produce the governing class.

The two young men, coming out of the water as she went in, had large shoulders and empty faces. She had a smile for them that was no more than they deserved – that must do until she chose one to be the father of her children and gave herself up to destiny. Until then – Henry Marston was glad about her as her arms, like flying fish, clipped the water in a crawl, as her body spread in a swan dive or doubled in a jackknife from the springboard and her head appeared from the depth, jauntily flipping the damp hair away.

The two young men passed near.

'They push water,' Choupette said, 'then they go elsewhere and push other water. They pass months in France and they couldn't tell you the name of the President. They are parasites such as Europe has not known in a hundred years.'

But Henry had stood up abruptly, and now all the people on the beach were suddenly standing up. Something had happened out there in the fifty yards between the deserted raft and the shore. The bright head showed upon the surface; it did not flip water now, but called: '*Au secours!* Help!' in a feeble and frightened voice.

'Henry!' Choupette cried. 'Stop! Henry!'

The beach was almost deserted at noon, but Henry and several others were sprinting toward the sea; the two young Americans heard, turned and sprinted after them. There was a frantic little time with half a dozen bobbing heads in the water. Choupette, still clinging to her parasol, but managing to wring her hands at the same time, ran up and down the beach crying: 'Henry! Henry!'

Now there were more helping hands, and then two swelling groups around prostrate figures on the shore. The young fellow who pulled in the girl brought her around in a minute or so, but they had more trouble getting the water out of Henry, who had never learned to swim.

II

'This is the man who didn't know whether he could swim, because he'd never tried.'

Henry got up from his sun chair, grinning. It was next morning, and the saved girl had just appeared on the beach with her brother. She smiled back at Henry, brightly casual, appreciative rather than grateful.

'At the very least, I owe it to you to teach you how,' she said.

'I'd like it. I decided that in the water yesterday, just before I went down the tenth time.'

'You can trust me. I'll never again eat chocolate ice cream before going in.'

As she went on into the water, Choupette asked: 'How long do you think we'll stay here? After all, this life wearies one.'

'We'll stay till I can swim. And the boys too.'

'Very well. I saw a nice bathing suit in two shades of blue for fifty francs that I will buy you this afternoon.'

Feeling a little paunchy and unhealthily white, Henry, holding his sons by the hand, took his body into the water. The breakers leaped at him, staggering him, while the boys yelled with ecstasy; the returning water curled threateningly around his feet as it hurried back to sea. Farther out, he stood waist deep with other intimidated souls, watching the people dive from the raft tower, hoping the girl would come to fulfill her promise, and somewhat embarrassed when she did.

'I'll start with your eldest. You watch and then try it by yourself.'

He floundered in the water. It went into his nose and started a raw stinging; it blinded him; it lingered afterward in his ears, rattling back and forth like pebbles for hours. The sun discovered him, too, peeling long strips of parchment from his shoulders, blistering his back so that he lay in a feverish agony for several nights. After a week he swam, painfully, pantingly, and not very far. The girl   37 taught him a sort of crawl, for he saw that the breast stroke was an obsolete device that lingered on with the inept and the old. Choupette caught him regarding his tanned face in the mirror with a sort of fascination, and the youngest boy contracted some sort of mild skin infection in the sand that retired him from competition. But one day Henry battled his way desperately to the float and drew himself up on it with his last breath.

'That being settled,' he told the girl, when he could speak, 'I can leave St Jean tomorrow.'

'I'm sorry.'

'What will you do now?'

'My brother and I are going to Antibes; there's swimming there all through October. Then Florida.'

'And swim?' he asked with some amusement.

'Why, yes. We'll swim.'

'Why do you swim?'

'To get clean,' she answered surprisingly.

'Clean from what?'

She frowned. 'I don't know why I said that. But it feels clean in the sea.'

'Americans are too particular about that,' he commented.

'How could anyone be?'

'I mean we've got too fastidious even to clean up our messes.'

'I don't know.'

'But tell me why you —' He stopped himself in surprise.

He had been about to ask her to explain a lot of other things – to say what was clean and unclean, what was worth knowing and what was only words – to open up a new gate to life. Looking for a last time into her eyes, full of cool secrets, he realized how much he was going to miss these mornings, without knowing whether it was the girl who interested him or what she represented of his ever-new, ever-changing country.

'All right,' he told Choupette that night. 'We'll leave tomorrow.'

'For Paris?'

'For America.'

'You mean I'm to go too? And the children?'

'Yes.'

'But that's absurd,' she protested. 'Last time it cost more than we spend in six months here. And then there were only three of us. Now that we've managed to get ahead at last —'

'That's just it. I'm tired of getting ahead on your skimping and saving and going without dresses. I've got to make more money. American men are incomplete without money.'

'You mean we'll stay?'

'It's very possible.'

They looked at each other, and against her will, Choupette understood. For eight years, by a process of ceaseless adaptation, he had lived her life, substituting for the moral confusion of his own country, the tradition, the wisdom, the sophistication of France. After that matter in Paris, it had seemed the bigger part to understand and to forgive, to cling to the home as something apart from the vagaries of love. Only now, glowing with a good health that he had not experienced for years, did he discover his true reaction. It had released him. For all his sense of loss, he possessed again the masculine self he had handed over to the keeping of a wise little Provençal girl eight years ago.

She struggled on for a moment.

'You've got a good position and we really have plenty of money. You know we can live cheaper here.'

'The boys are growing up now, and I'm not sure I want to educate them in France.'

'But that's all decided,' she wailed. 'You admit yourself that education in America is superficial and full of silly fads. Do you want them to be like those two dummies on the beach?'

'Perhaps I was thinking more of myself, Choupette. Men just out of college who brought their letters of credit into the bank eight years ago, travel about with ten-thousand-dollar cars now. I didn't use to care. I used to tell myself that I had a better place to escape to, just because, we knew that lobster armoricaine was really lobster américaine. Perhaps I haven't that feeling any more.'

She stiffened. 'If that's it —'

40   'It's up to you. We'll make a new start.'

Choupette thought for a moment. 'Of course my sister can take over the apartment.'

'Of course.' He waxed enthusiastic. 'And there are sure to be things that'll tickle you – we'll have a nice car, for instance, and one of those electric ice boxes, and all sorts of funny machines to take the place of servants. It won't be bad. You'll learn to play golf and talk about children all day. Then there are the movies.'

Choupette groaned.

'It's going to be pretty awful at first,' he admitted, 'but there are still a few good nigger cooks, and we'll probably have two bathrooms.'

'I am unable to use more than one at a time.'

'You'll learn.'

A month afterward, when the beautiful white island floated toward them in the Narrows, Henry's throat grew constricted with the rest and he wanted to cry out to Choupette and all foreigners, 'Now, you see!'

III

Almost three years later, Henry Marston walked out of his office in the Calumet Tobacco Company and along the hall to Judge Waterbury's suite. His face was older, with a suspicion of grimness, and a slight irrepressible heaviness of body was not concealed by his white linen suit.

'Busy, judge?'

'Come in, Henry.'

'I'm going to the shore tomorrow to swim off this weight. I wanted to talk to you before I go.'

'Children going too?'

'Oh, sure.'

'Choupette'll go abroad, I suppose.'

'Not this year. I think she's coming with me, if she doesn't stay here in Richmond.'

The judge thought: 'There isn't a doubt but that he knows everything.' He waited.

'I wanted to tell you, judge, that I'm resigning the end of September.'

'You're quitting, Henry?'

'Not exactly. Walter Ross wants to come home; let me take his place in France.'

'Boy, do you know what we pay Walter Ross?'

'Seven thousand.'

'And you're getting twenty-five.'

'You've probably heard I've made something in the market,' said Henry deprecatingly.

'I've heard everything between a hundred thousand and half a million.'

'Somewhere in between.'

'Then why a seven-thousand-dollar job? Is Choupette homesick?'

'No, I think Choupette likes it over here. She's adapted herself amazingly.'

'He knows,' the judge thought. 'He wants to get away.'

After Henry had gone, he looked up at the portrait of his grandfather on the wall. In those days the matter would have been simpler. Dueling pistols in the old Wharton meadow at dawn. It would be to Henry's advantage if things were like that today.

Henry's chauffeur dropped him in front of a Georgian house in a new suburban section. Leaving his hat in the hall, he went directly out on the side veranda.

From the swaying canvas swing Choupette looked up with a polite smile. Save for a certain alertness of feature and a certain indefinable knack of putting things on, she might have passed for an American. Southernisms overlay her French accent with a quaint charm; there were still college boys who rushed her like a débutante at the Christmas dances.

Henry nodded at Mr Charles Wiese, who occupied a wicker chair, with a gin fizz at his elbow.

'I want to talk to you,' he said, sitting down.

Wiese's glance and Choupette's crossed quickly before coming to rest on him.

'You're free, Wiese,' Henry said. 'Why don't you and Choupette get married?'

Choupette sat up, her eyes flashing.

'Now wait.' Henry turned back to Wiese. 'I've been letting this thing drift for about a year now, while I got my financial affairs in shape. But this last brilliant idea of yours makes me feel a little uncomfortable, a little sordid, and I don't want to feel that way.'

43

'Just what do you mean?' Wiese inquired.

'On my last trip to New York you had me shadowed. I presume it was with the intention of getting divorce evidence against me. It wasn't a success.'

'I don't know where you got such an idea in your head, Marston; you —'

'Don't lie!'

'Suh —' Wiese began, but Henry interrupted impatiently:

'Now don't "Suh" me, and don't try to whip yourself up into a temper. You're not talking to a scared picker full of hookworm. I don't want a scene; my emotions aren't sufficently involved. I want to arrange a divorce.'

'Why do you bring it up like this?' Choupette cried, breaking into French. 'Couldn't we talk of it alone, if you think you have so much against me?'

'Wait a minute; this might as well be settled now,' Wiese said. 'Choupette does want a divorce. Her life with you is unsatisfactory, and the only reason she has kept on is because she's an idealist. You don't seem to appreciate that fact, but it's true; she couldn't bring herself to break up her home.'

'Very touching.' Henry looked at Choupette with bitter amusement. 'But let's come down to facts. I'd like to close up this matter before I go back to France.'

Again Wiese and Choupette exchanged a look.

'It ought to be simple,' Wiese said. 'Choupette doesn't want a cent of your money.'

'I know. What she wants is the children. The answer is, You can't have the children.'

'How perfectly outrageous!' Choupette cried. 'Do you imagine for a minute I'm going to give up my children?'

'What's your idea, Marston?' demanded Wiese. 'To take them back to France and make them expatriates like yourself?'

'Hardly that. They're entered for St Regis School and then for Yale. And I haven't any idea of not letting them see their mother whenever she so desires – judging from the past two years, it won't be often. But I intend to have their entire legal custody.'

'Why?' they demanded together.

'Because of the home.'

'What the devil do you mean?'

'I'd rather apprentice them to a trade than have them brought up in the sort of home yours and Choupette's is going to be.'

There was a moment's silence. Suddenly Choupette picked up her glass, dashed the contents at Henry and collapsed on the settee, passionately sobbing.

Henry dabbed at his face with his handerkerchief and stood up.

'I was afraid of that,' he said, 'but I think I've made my position clear.'

He went up to his room and lay down on the bed. In a thousand wakeful hours during the past year he had fought over in his mind the problem of keeping his boys without taking those legal measures against Choupette that he could not bring himself to take. He knew that she wanted the children only because without them she would be suspect, even *déclassée*, to her family in France; but with that quality of detachment peculiar to old stock, Henry recognized this as a perfectly legitimate move. Furthermore, no public scandal must touch the mother of his sons – it was this that had rendered his challenge so ineffectual this afternoon.

When difficulties became insurmountable, inevitable, Henry sought surcease in exercise. For three years, swimming had been a sort of refuge, and he turned to it as one man to music or another to drink. There was a point when he would resolutely stop thinking and go to the Virginia coast for a week to wash his mind in the water. Far out past the breakers he could survey the green-and-brown line of the Old Dominion with the pleasant impersonality of a porpoise. The burden of his wretched marriage fell away with the buoyant tumble of his body among the swells, and he would begin to move in a child's dream of space. Sometimes remembered playmates of his youth swam with him; sometimes, with his two sons beside him, he seemed to be setting off along the bright pathway to the moon. Americans, he liked to say, should be born with fins, and perhaps they were – perhaps money was a form of fin. In England property begot a strong place sense, but Americans, restless and with shallow roots, needed fins and wings. There was even a recurrent idea in America about an education that would leave out history and the past, that should be a sort of equipment for aerial adventure, weighed down by none of the stowaways of inheritance or tradition.

Thinking of this in the water the next afternoon brought Henry's mind to the children; he turned and at a slow trudgen started back toward shore. Out of condition, he rested, panting, at the raft, and glancing up, he saw familiar eyes. In a moment he was talking with the girl he had tried to rescue four years ago.

He was overjoyed. He had not realized how vividly he remembered her. She was a Virginian — he might have guessed it abroad — the laziness, the apparent casualness that masked an unfailing courtesy and attention; a good form devoid of forms was based on kindness and consideration. Hearing her name for the first time, he recognized it — an Eastern Shore name, 'good' as his own.

Lying in the sun, they talked like old friends, not about races and manners and the things that Henry brooded over Choupette, but rather as if they naturally agreed about those things; they talked about what they liked themselves and about what was fun. She showed him a sitting-down, standing-up dive from the high springboard, and he emulated her inexpertly — that was fun. They talked about eating soft-shelled crabs, and she told him how, because of the curious acoustics of the water, one could lie here and be diverted by conversations on the hotel porch. They tried it and heard two ladies over their tea say:

'Now, at the Lido —'

'Now, at Asbury Park —'

'Oh, my dear, he just scratched and scratched all night; he just scratched and scratched —'

'My dear, at Deauville —'

'— scratched and scratched all night.'

After a while the sea got to be that very blue color of four o'clock, and the girl told him how, at nineteen, she had been divorced from a Spaniard who locked her in the hotel suite when he went out at night.

'It was one of those things,' she said lightly. 'But speaking more cheerfully, how's your beautiful wife? And the boys – did they learn to float? Why can't you all dine with me tonight?'

'I'm afraid I won't be able to,' he said, after a moment's hesitation. He must do nothing, however trivial, to furnish Choupette weapons, and with a feeling of disgust, it occurred to him that he was possibly being watched this afternoon. Nevertheless, he was glad of his caution when she unexpectedly arrived at the hotel for dinner that night.

After the boys had gone to bed, they faced each other over coffee on the hotel veranda.

'Will you kindly explain why I'm not entitled to a half share in my own children?' Choupette began. 'It is not like you to be vindictive, Henry.'

It was hard for Henry to explain. He told her again that she could have the children when she wanted them, but that he must exercise entire control over them because of certain old-fashioned convictions – watching her face grow harder, minute by minute, he saw there was no use, and broke off. She made a scornful sound.

'I wanted to give you a chance to be reasonable before Charles arrives.'

Henry sat up. 'Is he coming here this evening?'

'Happily. And I think perhaps your selfishness is going to have a jolt, Henry. You're not dealing with a woman now.'

When Wiese walked out on the porch an hour later, Henry saw that his pale lips were like chalk; there was a deep flush on his forehead and hard confidence in his eyes. He was cleared for action and he wasted no time. 'We've got something to say to each other, suh, and since I've got a motorboat here, perhaps that'd be the quietest place to say it.'

Henry nodded coolly; five minutes later the three of them were headed out into Hampton Roads on the wide fairway of the moonlight. It was a tranquil evening, and half a mile from shore Wiese cut down the engine to a mild throbbing, so that they seemed to drift without will or direction through the bright water. His voice broke the stillness abruptly:

'Marston, I'm going to talk to you straight from the shoulder. I love Choupette and I'm not apologizing for it. These things have happened before in this world. I guess you understand that. The only difficulty is this matter of the custody of Choupette's children. You seem determined to try and take them away from the mother that bore them and raised them' – Wiese's words became more clearly articulated, as if they came from a wider mouth – 'but you left one thing out of your calculations, and that's me. Do you happen to realize that at this moment I'm one of the richest men in Virginia?'

'I've heard as much.'

'Well, money is power, Marston. I repeat, suh, money is power.'

'I've heard that too. In fact, you're a bore, Wiese.' Even by the moon Henry could see the crimson deepen on his brow.

'You'll hear it again, suh. Yesterday you took us by surprise and I was unprepared for your brutality to Choupette. But this morning I received a letter from Paris that puts the matter in a new light. It is a statement by a specialist in mental diseases, declaring you to be of unsound mind, and unfit to have the custody of children. The specialist is the one who attended you in your nervous breakdown four years ago.'

Henry laughed incredulously, and looked at Choupette, half expecting her to laugh, too, but she had turned her face away, breathing quickly through parted lips. Suddenly he realized that Wiese was telling the truth – that by some extraordinary bribe he had obtained such a document and fully intended to use it.

For a moment Henry reeled as if from a material blow. He listened to his own voice saying, 'That's the most ridiculous thing I ever heard,' and to Wiese's answer: 'They don't always tell people when they have mental troubles.'

Suddenly Henry wanted to laugh, and the terrible instant when he had wondered if there could be some shred of truth in the allegation passed. He turned to Choupette, but again she avoided his eyes.

'How could you, Choupette?'

'I want my children,' she began, but Wiese broke in quickly:

'If you'd been halfway fair, Marston, we wouldn't have resorted to this step.'

'Are you trying to pretend you arranged this scurvy trick since yesterday afternoon?'

'I believe in being prepared, but if you had been reasonable; in fact, if you will be reasonable, this opinion needn't be used.' His voice became suddenly almost paternal, almost kind: 'Be wise, Marston. On your side there's an obstinate prejudice; on mine there are forty million dollars. Don't fool yourself. Let me repeat, Marston, that money is power. You were abroad so long that perhaps you're inclined to forget that fact. Money made this country, built its great and glorious cities, created its industries, covered it with an iron network of railroads. It's money that harnesses the forces of Nature, creates the machine and makes it go when money says go, and stop when money says stop.'

As though interpreting this as a command, the engine

gave forth a sudden hoarse sound and came to rest.

'What is it?' demanded Choupette.

'It's nothing.' Wiese pressed the self-starter with his foot. 'I repeat, Marston, that money — The battery is dry. One minute while I spin the wheel.'

He spun it for the best part of fifteen minutes while the boat meandered about in a placid little circle.

'Choupette, open that drawer behind you and see if there isn't a rocket.'

A touch of panic had crept into her voice when she answered that there was no rocket. Wiese eyed the shore tentatively.

'There's no use in yelling; we must be half a mile out. We'll just have to wait here until someone comes along.'

'We won't wait here,' Henry remarked.

'Why not?'

'We're moving toward the bay. Can't you tell? We're moving out with the tide.'

'That's impossible!' said Choupette sharply.

'Look at those two lights on shore — one passing the other now. Do you see?'

'Do something!' she wailed, and then, in a burst of French: 'Ah, c'est épouvantable! N'est-ce pas qu'il y a quelque chose qu'on peut faire?'

The tide was running fast now, and the boat was drifting down the Roads with it toward the sea. The vague blots of two ships passed them, but at a distance, and there was no answer to their hail. Against the western sky a lighthouse blinked, but it was impossible to guess how near to it they would pass.

'It looks as if all our difficulties would be solved for us,' Henry said.

'What difficulties?' Choupette demanded. 'Do you mean there's nothing to be done? Can you sit there and just float away like this?'

'It may be easier on the children, after all.' He winced as Choupette began to sob bitterly, but he said nothing. A ghostly idea was taking shape in his mind.

'Look here, Marston. Can you swim?' demanded Wiese, frowning.

'Yes, but Choupette can't.'

'I can't either – I didn't mean that. If you could swim in and get to a telephone, the coast-guard people would send for us.'

Henry surveyed the dark, receding shore.

'It's too far,' he said.

'You can try!' said Choupette.

Henry shook his head.

'Too risky. Besides, there's an outside chance that we'll be picked up.'

The lighthouse passed them, far to the left and out of earshot. Another one, the last, loomed up half a mile away.

'We might drift to France like that man Gerbault,' Henry remarked. 'But then, of course, we'd be expatriates – and Wiese wouldn't like that, would you, Wiese?'

Wiese, fussing frantically with the engine, looked up.

'See what you can do with this,' he said.

'I don't know anything about mechanics,' Henry answered. 'Besides, this solution of our difficulties grows on me. Just suppose you were dirty dog enough to use that statement and got the children because of it – in that case I wouldn't have much impetus to go on living. We're all failures – I as head of my household. Choupette as a wife and a mother, and you, Wiese, as a human being. It's just as well that we go out of life together.'

'This is no time for a speech, Marston.'

'Oh, yes, it's a fine time. How about a little more house-organ oratory about money being power?'

Choupette sat rigid in the bow; Wiese stood over the engine, biting nervously at his lips.

'We're going to pass that lighthouse very close.' An idea suddenly occurred to him. 'Couldn't you swim to that, Marston?'

'Of course he could!' Choupette cried.

Henry looked at it tentatively.

'I might. But I won't.'

'You've got to!'

Again he flinched at Choupette's weeping; simultaneously he saw the time had come.

'Everything depends on one small point,' he said rapidly. 'Wiese, have you got a fountain pen?'

'Yes. What for?'

'If you'll write and sign about two hundred words at my dictation, I'll swim to the lighthouse and get help.

Otherwise, so help me God, we'll drift out to sea! And you better decide in about one minute.'

'Oh, anything!' Choupette broke out frantically. 'Do what he says, Charles; he means it. He always means what he says. Oh, please don't wait!'

'I'll do what you want' – Wiese's voice was shaking – 'only, for God's sake, go on. What is it you want – an agreement about the children? I'll give you my personal word of honor —'

'There's no time for humor,' said Henry savagely. 'Take this piece of paper and write.'

The two pages that Wiese wrote at Henry's dictation relinquished all lien on the children thence and forever for himself and Choupette. When they had affixed trembling signatures Wiese cried:

'Now go, for God's sake, before it's too late!'

'Just one thing more: The certificate from the doctor.'

'I haven't it here.'

'You lie.'

Wiese took it from his pocket.

'Write across the bottom that you paid so much for it, and sign your name to that.'

A minute later, stripped to his underwear, and with the papers in an oiled-silk tobacco pouch suspended from his neck, Henry dived from the side of the boat and struck out toward the light.

The waters leaped up at him for an instant, but after the first shock it was all warm and friendly, and the small 55 murmur of the waves was an encouragement. It was the longest swim he had ever tried, and he was straight from the city, but the happiness in his heart buoyed him up. Safe now, and free. Each stroke was stronger for knowing that his two sons, sleeping back in the hotel, were safe from what he dreaded. Divorced from her own country, Choupette had picked the things out of American life that pandered best to her own self-indulgence. That, backed by a court decree, she should be permitted to hand on this preposterous moral farrago to his sons was unendurable. He would have lost them forever.

Turning on his back, he saw that already the motorboat was far away, the blinding light was nearer. He was very tired. If one let go – and, in the relaxation from strain, he felt an alarming impulse to let go – one died very quickly and painlessly, and all these problems of hate and bitterness disappeared. But he felt the fate of his sons in the oiled-silk pouch about his neck, and with a convulsive effort he turned over again and concentrated all his energies on his goal.

Twenty minutes later he stood shivering and dripping in the signal room while it was broadcast out to the coast patrol that a launch was drifting in the bay.

'There's not much danger without a storm,' the keeper said. 'By now they've probably struck a cross current from the river and drifted into Peyton Harbor.'

'Yes,' said Henry, who had come to this coast for three summers. 'I knew that too.'

In October, Henry left his sons in school and embarked on the Majestic for Europe. He had come home as to a generous mother and had been profusely given more than he asked — money, release from an intolerable situation, and the fresh strength to fight for his own. Watching the fading city, the fading shore, from the deck of the Majestic, he had a sense of overwhelming gratitude and of gladness that America was there, that under the ugly débris of industry the rich land still pushed up, incorrigibly lavish and fertile, and that in the heart of the leaderless people the old generosities and devotions fought on, breaking out sometimes in fanaticism and excess, but indomitable and undefeated. There was a lost generation in the saddle at the moment, but it seemed to him that the men coming on, the men of the war, were better; and all his old feeling that America was a bizarre accident, a sort of historical sport, had gone forever. The best of America was the best of the world.

Going down to the purser's office, he waited until a fellow passenger was through at the window. When she turned, they both started, and he saw it was the girl.

'Oh, hello!' she cried. 'I'm glad you're going! I was just asking when the pool opened. The great thing about this ship is that you can always get a swim.'

'Why do you like to swim?' he demanded.

'You always ask me that.' She laughed.

'Perhaps you'd tell me if we had dinner together tonight.'

But when, in a moment, he left her he knew that she could never tell him – she or another. France was a land, England was a people, but America, having about it still that quality of the idea, was harder to utter – it was the graves at Shiloh and the tired, drawn, nervous faces of its great men, and the country boys dying in the Argonne for a phrase that was empty before their bodies withered. It was a willingness of the heart.

PHOENIX 60P PAPERBACKS

HISTORY/BIOGRAPY/TRAVEL
The Empire of Rome A.D. 98–190 *Edward Gibbon*
The Prince *Machiavelli*
The Alan Clark Diaries: Thatcher's Fall *Alan Clark*
Churchill: Embattled Hero *Andrew Roberts*
The French Revolution *E.J. Hobsbawm*
Voyage Around the Horn *Joshua Slocum*
The Great Fire of London *Samuel Pepys*
Utopia *Thomas More*
The Holocaust *Paul Johnson*
Tolstoy and History *Isaiah Berlin*

SCIENCE AND PHILOSOPHY
A Guide to Happiness *Epicurus*
Natural Selection *Charles Darwin*
Science, Mind & Cosmos *John Brockman, ed.*
Zarathustra *Friedrich Nietzsche*
God's Utility Function *Richard Dawkins*
Human Origins *Richard Leakey*
Sophie's World: The Greek Philosophers *Jostein Gaarder*
The Rights of Woman *Mary Wollstonecraft*
The Communist Manifesto *Karl Marx & Friedrich Engels*
Birds of Heaven *Ben Okri*

FICTION
Riot at Misri Mandi *Vikram Seth*
The Time Machine *H. G. Wells*
Love in the Night *F. Scott Fitzgerald*

The Murders in the Rue Morgue *Edgar Allen Poe*
The Necklace *Guy de Maupassant*
You Touched Me *D. H. Lawrence*
The Mabinogion *Anon*
Mowgli's Brothers *Rudyard Kipling*
Shancarrig *Maeve Binchy*
A Voyage to Lilliput *Jonathan Swift*

POETRY
Songs of Innocence and Experience *William Blake*
The Eve of Saint Agnes *John Keats*
High Waving Heather *The Brontes*
Sailing to Byzantium *W. B. Yeats*
I Sing the Body Electric *Walt Whitman*
The Ancient Mariner *Samuel Taylor Coleridge*
Intimations of Immortality *William Wordsworth*
Palgrave's Golden Treasury of Love Poems *Francis Palgrave*
Goblin Market *Christina Rossetti*
Fern Hill *Dylan Thomas*

LITERATURE OF PASSION
Don Juan *Lord Byron*
From Bed to Bed *Catullus*
Satyricon *Petronius*
Love Poems *John Donne*
Portrait of a Marriage *Nigel Nicolson*
The Ballad of Reading Gaol *Oscar Wilde*
Love Sonnets *William Shakespeare*
Fanny Hill *John Cleland*
The Sexual Labyrinth (for women) *Alina Reyes*
Close Encounters (for men) *Alina Reyes*